Saved by
grace

Vongai Monica Mujakachi

CgHope Publications | ZIMBABWE

2019

ISBN 978-0-7974-9293-6
EAN 9780797492936

Saved By Grcae by Vongai Monica Mujakachi

Copyright © 2019 CgHope Publications

Email: cghopepublications@outlook.com

Call: +263 (0) 783 484 266
+263 (0) 736 315 639

CgHope
Publications

Digitally published by CgHope Publications
in Bulawayo, Zimbabwe.

Unless or otherwise stated, all scriptural quotations are
from the King James Version of the Bible.

All possible efforts were made by CgHope Publications to
secure permission and ensure proper credit was given for
every entry within this book.

DEDICATION

To everyone who seeks to know God better.

ACKNOWELDGEMENT

- ○ To my beloved parents for being there for me.
- ○ To Xesha Khumalo, my publisher, for his continued support and keeping me going in my journey of writing. A true friend indeed!
- ○ To my friends: Beauty Mutengo and Yvet Mabuto.

CONTENTS

INTRODUCTION

'Saved By Grace' is an imprint of God's love. He has done great things in our lives, not because of our works, but because of His grace.

When we were bound by troubles and plagued with condemnation; but He saved us. With His grace bestowed upon us; we are in awe because we once lived without direction—we were walking graves.

Therefore, we should not take His grace for granted, but we should walk and grow in it. The book also serves to comfort and give hope to those who have lost hope. It also praises the mighty God because of His unconditional love and mercy.

Come, O ye Sinner

Countless times you have said.

Countless times you have thought.

Countless times you have done the wrong.

You have turned your back and even mocked His word.

In your eyes, you were wise.

Foolishness became wisdom to you.

You remained ignorant.

He watched you as you dragged yourself.

Away from His loving and protective arms.

The devil watched you like a hawk.

With His devilish smile, he was content.

Now that you were alone.

He could easily snarl and snatch you.

You became his playground.

Your mind—his workshop.

Your body—his temple of filthiness.

He left you all alone.

Chained in a dungeon.

Now you regret why you never listened to the still small voice.

You feel like there is no other way to your freedom.

You feel like it's over.

Saul of Tarsus was a terror to the church.

A murder hunting down Christians.

Jesus Christ saved him.

Paul became his name,

And the footsteps of Christ, He followed.

Come, O ye sinner.

God will embrace you.

Just like the lost sheep.

With open arms He will take you back.

Just like the lost son.

Come, O ye sinner!

Tell it to Jesus

Tell your worries to men.
Tell your problems to men.
The next thing,
It will be all over the world.
Worse than it was.

Tell your worries to men.
Tell your problems to men.
You might be telling your enemy.
You will shed more tears.
As the smiles at your back.

Tell your worries to man.
Tell your problems to man.
They pretend as if they care,
But behind your back they smile.

Kneel down and tell it to Jesus.
He is ever ready to listen to you.
Ever ready to change your mess to a message.
Tell it Jesus, He has every answer that you need.
Tell it to Jesus.

Hearing and Doing

Indeed there is no other way,

To be happy in Jesus, than to hear and do His word.

If you hear the word of God and do it,

You would have obeyed Him.

His word benefits the hearers.

His mercies befall those who are obedient.

The Lord has given us so much, which we are thankful for.

Our words will never be sufficient to show our gratitude.

Let us hear His word and live it.

Jonah disobeyed God.

Told what to do,

He decided to run away.

In the boat, God roused a storm.

All this was because Jonah had disobeyed.

Jonah was swallowed alive by a whale.

The fish spit him out on a dry land after three days,

When he repented from his wicked ways.

Noah obeyed God by building an ark.

He was saved with his family.

Through hearing and acting upon God's word, King Solomon
prospered in wealth and in wisdom.
Obey the Lord for the rest of your life,
And you shall eat the fruits of obedience.

Prayer and Faith

No one is safe for a day without prayer and faith.

To have faith, you must know God.

The knowledge of God comes through reading His word.

Your faith is therefore, a product of knowledge of His word.

You pray because you have faith that God is alive.

Your relationship with God is strengthened through prayer.

Abraham had faith.

Up the mountain Moriah—he had faith that God would provide

a ram for the sacrifice.

The centurion had faith and his servant was healed.

With faith, the paralyzed man was healed.

Elijah prayed for the rain and it came down.

Through prayer Shadrech, Misheck and Abednigo were saved

when they were cast in the fiery furnace.

When Daniel was thrown in the den of lions he prayed and he

was not harmed.

Pray from a clean heart.

For God answers the prayer of the righteous.

If we remain resolute in prayer and faith,

We will witness in our lives progress.

The journey is long

This journey is so long, oh God!
I want you by my side all the time.
Alone l am afraid.
Alone l am afraid to face this world.

In what l do.
In what l think.
In what l say.
I want you to be happy.

Plant love deep down in my heart.
So that l can never sin again.
Purify my heart.
Let your words not escape my mouth.

Whenever l get lost,
Show me the way to paradise.
The journey is long; walk with me!

We need Jesus

In a world of many evils,

And the enemy's wicked devises.

What do 1 need? What do 1 do?

When you are crying every day,

Nobody by your side to wash away the pain.

When we are all in the darkness.

Facing all the harshness.

When we can't see the light,

To lighten our path.

I need Jesus,

The way and the light.

You need Jesus,

The comforter and protector.

We all need Jesus,

The savior.

We need Jesus!

Does God really care

Tears have become the order of the day.

For the widows and orphans.

Looking above, questions they ask—

Does God really care?

Our hearts are left in pain,

When our beloved ones depart.

Left with memories, we ask—

Does God really care?

As our lives get horrendously twisted.

When misfortunes become so common.

Paining us now and again.

Does God really care?

God does really care.

"All things work together for good,

To them that love God," says the His word.

For there is a reason for everything.

Accept God's grace,

And He will deliver you from all your miseries.

The Almighty God will never allow, either good or bad,

To happen to you, without His permission.

God is love, He loves us.

And yes He does care.

I want to be there

I want to be there, singing the songs of the Almighty God.
I want to be there in paradise, singing His songs.

I will face everything the: good and the bad,
So I can make it in paradise.
When I fall I will rise up to fight, with the strength bestowed
upon me,
I will conquer!

I become A Victor.

Amazing God.

You are amazing

You raise me high, whenever I fall.

You give me strength, whenever I'm weak.

When I face temptations.

You create a way for me to overcome.

I become a victor.

When I am afraid,

You sooth me.

"Do not be afraid," you tell me.

I become bold and face my fears.

I become a victor.

When sickness hovers.

When they say it's over,

You show yourself as the greatest physician.

You heal me,

And I become a victor.

When I have nothing,

They watch and think that I will starve.

You provide and leave me lacking nothing.

I become a victor.

Sadness and pain.

The world born of sin.

Difficulties and disappointments crossing my path.

You bring joy and happiness.

I become a victor.

I lack nothing, because you are there.

You watch over me day and night.

I feel safe, though I'm in this sin-congested world,

All because you are there.

How I love you, oh, God!

I will praise you.

Many times I may fail you,

But I will keep on fighting;

To make you happy.

For in and with you.

I become a victor.

I will praise Thee

You heard me cry.

Took me out of the horrible pit.

You heard me cry,

And cleansed my soul.

Unworthy I was, but still you sent your Son.

He died for my sins.

Now I'm set free.

I give you all the glory, you are worth of all the praise.

I will worship you wholly,

For the rest of my life.

Unto you I lift my eyes.

I will praise you.

I will sing of your mercy and justice;

I will praise you.

I will serve you with gladness.

I seek thy strength

Give me a pure heart Oh God.

So l can shun every sin.

My spirit and my flesh.

These two are in a battlefield.

Lord purify my heart.

My flesh loves the world,

Yet my spirit yearns and is thirsting for your word.

I ask for strength,

To fight evil thoughts.

My mind wanders everywhere.

It devises evil.

Revenge it plans.

I seek your strength, oh, merciful God!

I know I have to forgive,

I know pride should depart.

Yet I'm boastful.

I accommodate bitterness in my heart.

I seek strength,

To fight the lusts of the flesh.

I seek strength, so that I may be led by the Spirit.

So the fruits of the Spirit may manifest in my life.

Passersby

We came with nothing,

So shall we return with nothing.

We are travelers.

Just visitors

Nothing more than passersby.

We do not live forever,

Lest we forget.

One day we shall say goodbye.

Where will your soul go to?

The time is now, to make a choice—

Eternal life or eternal suffering.

Our days are numbered.

"Seek first the kingdom of God.

And all shall be given unto you,"

Thus says the Lord.

Are you taking stock of your life?

Are you watching where your feet step?

Surely we are passersby.

And when the day to leave the earth comes.

Will you be able to face the judgement day?
For the Lord rewards according to deeds.
In everything you do, bear in mind,
That we are merely passersby.

Go back

The days when you loved Him.

When you loved Him;

With all your heart,

Your mind,

Your strength,

When His word was your food,

And prayer your shield.

Close to Him, you were.

You even felt His presence.

When you prayed,

And felt that your prayer reached Him.

Unrighteous ways, you shunned.

His righteous paths you shined in.

You felt complete in His ways.

You ran well.

Who hindered you from obeying the truth?

Now you don't run.

You don't even walk,

Nor even crawl.

You have stopped, stuck standing.
You are now a church goer, not a Christian.
As for praying,
You seldom do and when you do,
It is not whole heartedly.
You have gone astray.
You sin and you don't mind.
His grace you now take for granted.

You cannot have fellowship with God,
And still walk in darkness.
If you do not practice the truth,
Then you are not in fellowship with Him.

Stand up;
Shake off the dust,
And walk in His light,
The way you did before.
Go back to those days.

Trust in thy Lord

When all the hope is lost.

When we no longer hope against hope.

When we seem lost and know not the way.

When the world goes against us.

Let us remember that God is able.

He is able to turn our sorrows to happiness.

He is able to wipe away our tears.

He is able to fight all our battles.

He is able to shower our lives with blessings,

For He is the Almighty God.

The Alpha and Omega.

Why then do you cry?

Why allow sadness to reign in your life?

Why fear the obstacles that Satan places in front of you?

Let prayer be your weapon. Stand firm and be unshakable.

Through trials, tribulations and tests let prayer be your weapon.

Let His word be on your mouth always.

Walk in His ways and build a relationship with Him.

Put your trust in Him, like Daniel in the den of lions.

Thrown in a den of lions, he trusted Him and was unharmed.

For He is the Almighty and able God.

I seek Thee

My weakness, you know.

Where stumble and fall.

Temptations, I give in to.

The unrighteous ways I fail to overcome,

All that, you know Lord.

I come before you.

Your presence, I seek;

So I can overcome,

Temptations and sins, I encounter.

What comes out of my mouth.

Is undesirable for your ears.

Help me tame my tongue.

Let it know how to praise you.

Let it know how to praise you.

Let goodness come out of it.

My mind is a battlefield.

The wrong thoughts uninvited, engulf me.

I try to fight, to shut these thoughts.

I fail and give in.

May you purify my mind.

So that pure thoughts may flow.

I know I should let go.

I know I should forgive and forget.

Forgiving takes ages.

Forgetting is impossible.

Bitterness still reside.

Pour in my heart the spirit of forgiveness.

As you forgive me countless times.

Give me the spirit of forgiving, those who wrong me.

I seek thee, oh, Lord.

He is able

Hope shattered.
Your life crumbling down.
As you lie down hopeless.
Helpless, with no voice to cry for help.

In a dark pit.
With darkness as your companion.
In your remorseful state.
That sad state.
He is able.

He is able to lift you up.
He is able to bring you a smile.
He is able to fight all your battles.
He is able, because He is a mighty God.

He is able to create something out of nothing,
And His grace abounds.
He is able to deliver,
He is able to fulfil His promises.

When she was past the age of bearing,

Sarah gave birth to a son, Isaac.

God is omnipotent and is able to do anything!

When He cometh

Will you be able to face him?

Or you will hide your face from Him?

There will be no witness, but just your works.

The unrighteous and evil shall run rampant.

He shall judge accordingly.

Satan, his demons and the unrighteous shall be thrown into the

lack of fire.

They will burn for eternity.

There will begin a glorious time.

No more death.

No more fear.

No more crying.

No more pain.

Just happiness.

Will you be able to stand before Him?—

When He cometh.

God'sGrace

A valley of tears; that was your daily life.

Full of misery, pain and strife.

Every trail wearied your soul.

You forgot that you could kneel and pray.

You felt empty, forsaken and lonely.

God showered you with His grace.

You were freed from your miserable life.

Perfect light, illuminated your way.

You received your salvation.

And became God's new creation.

You were saved by grace.

And now you can rise above all obstacles.

Fear and strife varnished from your life.

Grace will carry you.

Now all you have to do,

Is to grow each day,

In the power of God's grace.

He Finds A Way

Tears streaming down on my troubled face.
My mind going all places, seeking for solutions.
Sighing every minute. The burden is too much!
Awake in my sleep, because in dreams I'm still haunted.

A rocky, prickling path—will I reach my destiny?
I fail to hear the sweat voice, how ignorant!
Every step that I take I stumble and fall in this darkness.
Blinded and deceived by what I call wisdom;
The wisdom of men which cannot eradicate my burdens.

When all hope is lost, He appears by my side.
"Come hither my child,"
He whispers calmly. So bright, the light shines ahead.
He leads me with love and tenderness.
If only I had listened to His voice from the start.
I would have saved myself from all the pain,
And hurt. Indeed he finds a way.

Lord of Mercy

I shiver even when it's hot.

My heart is torn apart.

My life is crushing.

My world is breaking apart.

Hear my cry, oh, Lord of Mercy!

My enemies dance and celebrate.

A withered flower; such is my life.

Where is your God? They mock.

Answer me, oh, Lord of mercy!

I have no one to run to.

You are my shelter.

In all the storms of life.

You are my refuge.

Only you can break these chains.

Only you can set me free from these tribulations.

Oh, Lord of mercy!

I Wouldn't Be Here

Where do I begin?

Where do I start?

My heart is bubbling with joy.

My heart is full of thanks.

For if not for Him.

I wouldn't be here.

Had He not loved me.

Had He not sent His only Son Jesus Christ,

To die for my sins on the cross.

Surely, I wouldn't be here.

Then where will I be?

I would be in the mud.

Right where He picked me.

I would be in the deep pit.

Where no one would hear me,

Languishing in pain.

Right where He heard my voice.

And saved me with His grace.

I wouldn't be here;

Here in His house,

Where I lack nothing.

My life, He transformed for good.

My days, He richly blessed.

If not for Him,

I wouldn't be here.

Bubble-Gums

Our money, we spent on bubble-gums.

We would chew them until the taste was gone.

It was a frustration that the taste did not last long.

We had no choice, but to throw them away.

Such is the world.

This world is like a bubble gum.

Its sweetness is indeed deceitful—

It does not last.

We are going to leave its pleasures behind,

And take nothing with us, when we kiss goodbye.

Call it a 'bubble gum world'.

Why the do we let ourselves be fooled?

Why then do we turn back to the world?

The word of God is everlasting, forever it remains.

Take heed and embrace it.

Walk and grow in it,

For indeed it lasts forever.

Break up with the 'bubble gum world',

For it will take you nowhere, when you leave this world.

Empty_Life

I feel like a cadaver.

Yes, I'm still breathing,

But outside, I feel like an empty shell.

I am lost in the woods.

Countless questions torment me mercilessly.

How did I end up here?

In a pit, so deep and haunting.

I'm like a robot in everything that I do.

When will I walk away?

When will I leave this burdensome place?

A melancholic place.

Where no one shoved me in.

Darkness fills the place.

I'm now a prisoner.

At first I thought this was life,

But now I yearn for freedom.

I'm paralyzed by this empty life.

Blindness has disappeared,

And now I see the grave-mistakes I made.

The foolishness I attained through ignorance.

Now I know that without Jesus,

I will forever be servant;

A servant to this empty life.

Saved By Grace

You had lost all hope.

You had nowhere to go.

Your life was meaningless.

Then the Lord came in your life.

With His grace, He changed everything.

So you could see the light.

It was only His grace which saved you,

Not your works.

Until when?

Oh, you men of little faith.

I'm discombobulated with your extent of ignorance.

Why do you cling to your destructive ways?

You refuse to hearken to His word.

Foolishness harbors in your mind.

Seek wisdom whilst you can.

You have limited time.

You are just a visitor in this world,

Never forget that.

Never get carried away.

For how long are you going to be deaf?

For how long are you going to dine with the heartless?

Oh, beloved friend! For how long?

It's never too late to take a turn;

A turn to walk straight.

His arms are wide open for you,

For He is the God of mercy.

A Pure Heart

Pray without ceasing.

Read the bible on a daily basis.

Go to Church regularly.

Shout Hallelujah and Amen.

That is all useless,

If you lack a pure heart.

Sing songs of glory.

Preach the gospel of salvation.

Pay your tithes.

Give your offerings.

Without a pure heart,

You are doing nothing.

Let your heart be pure.

In the sight of the Lord,

Let your heart be pure.

Fill it with love.

Fill it with compassion.

Let your heart be pure.

My long home

I cannot acculturate.

They are in no accede with the Word of God.

And for that reason,

I will segregate myself.

I will remain distant to the walks of this world.

The zeal to quench my thirst.

A longing to belong, can no longer be ignored.

But deep down, I know I have to allow patience to reign.

I have never seen it, but I know one thing:

Its beauty is beyond imagination.

Suffering is non-existent.

Weeping is diminished,

Hunger and poverty are unheard of.

That is the life I will live in my long home.

Reach to you again

For your sake, I was afflicted.

Day and night, I call to you.

When will you hear me?

You have plugged logs in your ears.

Such that my voice is not heard to you.

You are sinking in the mud.

Your life is in shreds, bits and pieces of rags.

You look like an old man, yet you are young.

If only you could open your eyes,

You would see the joy that awaits you,

A blissful life ahead of you.

What comes out of your tongue is rotten.

Your thoughts are stale and stinking.

Blessed with hands, yet you steal without shame.

You ruin people's lives, oh, daughter!

When will you hear my voice?

Immorality resides deep within you.

You hurt them all: the young, old, married and the single.

Marriages are torn apart because of you.

You are ignorant of the destruction and havoc that you cause.

I would cry if I were you.

I would cry at the pit of my lungs for light.

Red as blood, are your sins,

Answer to my call and I will make them as white as snow.

Seek me and you will find me.

I am the same yesterday, today and forever.

I will always love you, for you are my child.

I am your Creator and you are my creation,

For that reason, I will reach to you again.

Walk with me

I have ran miles and miles,

Chasing the wind.

Not anymore!

I refuse to walk alone.

I thought I could make it on my own.

Everything is possible, if I work hard.

But it was all useless.

All the knowledge I earned.

My success is nowhere to be found,

If I am alone.

I call to you my redeemer.

I've made fatal mistakes.

I have ignored you.

My relationship with you lies in ruins.

A grave choice, I have made.

I call to you for salvation.

I confess today that you are my king.

Only you can save me Lord.

I will never get lost.

I will firmly build myself in faith,
And I will never lose hope.
If you walk with me.

Forgive me

Before your eyes I was a disgrace.

A sinner who was saved by your grace.

You enlightened my paths and blindness vanished.

From the dust you raised me.

Leaving my enemies filled with rage.

For you broke the chain

Free as a fly, everything I wanted you granted.

But slowly, I forgot you.

Slowly, I went out off the track.

Each day passing, meant a decrease in my prayer life.

I became lazy to feast on your word.

I forgot that I own nothing,

That I am something because of you.

My spirit I starred.

I grew ignorant, but I still saw myself wise.

Today I come before you with shame.

Forgive me, my Lord,

And help me to carry my cross,

Live and walk your way.

Help me to be steadfast in your word.

Close Friend

Who is your close friend?

Who do you open up to?

Who gives you advice?

Does your close friend lead you in a good way?

Or they push you into a pit?

It is better to be friendless,

Than to be surrounded by friends,

Who do nothing, but lead you astray.

Choose with care.

"He who walks with wise men will be wise, but the companion

of fools will be destroyed."

What role are they playing?

Are they helping you grow spiritually?

Or they are making you backslide!

Make God your close friend.

He does not laugh behind your back.

He does not pretend to love you.

Let Him be your rock and fortress.

Let him be your close friend.

Prayer

In prayer there is power.

Pray without ceasing.

Regardless of the obstacles you face.

Let prayer be your hiding cave.

In various storms of life,

Through prayer you will be a victor.

How then can you communicate with the creator?

How then will you praise and worship God?

If not through prayer.

Through trails, tribulations and tests;

Prayer is the weapon to use,

God is ready to listen to your prayer anytime.

Pray whole-heartedly to God.

Pour your heart to Him.

Cast all your burdens and he will carry them for you.

Indeed there is power in prayer!

Word of God

Flowers wither away.

People die.

The earth will pass away;

But the word of God,

Will stand.

For the Word of God is alive

It penetrating in our hearts,

And without it, we are worthless.

For it teaches and rebukes us.

It is the lamp to our feet,

Guiding us in righteousness

Let your ears be open to His Word.

And when you hear, obey;

And you will be saved!

BOOKS BY THE SAME AUTHOR

- o Songs Of Life by Vongai Monica Mujakachi, Copyright © 2017 CgHope Publications.

- o Choices We Make And Other Stories by Ntombizile Ncube & Vongai Monica Mujakachi, Copyright © 2018 CgHope Publications.

- o The Lost Generation by Zenzo Siziba & Vongai Monica Mujakachi, Copyright © 2018 CgHope Publications.